PROTECTING HIS BEST FRIEND'S DAUGHTER
SUNSET SECURITY BOOK FOUR

SADIE KING

PROTECTING HIS BEST FRIEND'S DAUGHTER

Twenty years of military discipline hasn't prepared me for one weekend with Amy...

Leo

Amy's the perfect woman. Sweet, funny, and curves that make my mouth water. Too bad she's my best friend's daughter and completely off limits.

When he asks me to protect her, he has no idea how far I'll go to keep her safe.

Amy may be forbidden to me, but I won't let any other man touch her.

Amy

It's only ever been Leo. Since he made me laugh when I was twelve years old, I've had a crush on him.

But he still sees me as a little girl.

When we're thrown together for the weekend, it's my chance to show him I'm more than a little girl. I'm a woman—his woman.

He thinks we should do the right thing. He thinks we can't be together.

Leo has a will of steel, and I'm determined to break him…

Protecting His Best Friend's Daughter is a forbidden love, age-gap, instalove romance featuring an OTT ex-military hero and the curvy woman he claims as his own.

Part of the Sunset Security series and set in the Sunset Coast world. Every story is a stand-alone, but best enjoyed together. No cliffhangers and always with a happily ever after.

DON'T MISS OUT!

Want to be the first to hear about new releases and special offers?

Follow Sadie King on BookBub to get an alert whenever she has a new release, preorder, or discount!

www.bookbub.com/authors/sadie-king

Copyright © 2023 by Sadie King.

All rights reserved.

No part of this book may be reproduced in any form or by any electronic or mechanical means, including information storage and retrieval systems, without written permission from the author, except for the use of brief quotations in a book review.

This is a work of fiction. Any resemblance to actual events, companies, locales or persons living or dead, are entirely coincidental.

Cover design by Designrans

www.authorsadieking.com

CONTENTS

1.	Amy	1
2.	Leo	8
3.	Amy	14
4.	Leo	21
5.	Amy	24
6.	Leo	30
7.	Amy	37
8.	Leo	43
9.	Leo	50
10.	Amy	56
	Epilogue	61
	What to read next	65
	Protecting His Ex-Wife	67
	Get your FREE Book	73
	Books by Sadie King	75
	About the Author	77

1
AMY

At the sound of the door sliding open, I look up from the computer. As the receptionist for Sunset Security, it's my job to greet new clients with a sunny smile and pleasant demeanor. But the smile freezes on my lips when I see who it is coming in the main entrance.

"I bought you a cappuccino." The boy holds up a takeout cup with coffee that I didn't ask for and probably won't drink.

I've got a reusable takeout mug sitting under the desk that I use whenever I want coffee from the cafe next door, which is hardly ever since Bronn got the good coffee machine installed in the kitchen.

But since the one time I bought a cappuccino from the shop next door, this boy's got it in his head that he's doing something nice for me by bringing over a free drink every day.

It would be sweet if it wasn't such an obvious excuse to stare at my boobs.

"Thank you."

I've been brought up too polite to refuse a gift, so I thank him and take the drink, which sloshes over the rim and burns my fingers.

The boy—I forget his name. James or Jaxon or Jamie? I don't want to ask because it would be rude considering he's been coming in here for the last two weeks. Whatever his name is, he leans on the reception desk and gives me a nervous smile.

"I, um…"

His eyes flick to my chest, making me wish I'd worn a high-neck blouse instead of the low-cut one I put on trying to get someone else's attention.

When his gaze comes back to mine, his pimply cheeks are tinged pink.

At least he has the decency to be embarrassed about getting caught staring at my chest.

"I, um… Do you want to have a coffee with me sometime?"

He's nervous and sweet, and his brown eyes look both terrified and hopeful.

He's not bad looking, if you like that kind of thing, with a thick head of sandy hair and clear, youthful skin. His face is clean shaven and smooth. There're no scars of experience or lines on his face.

He's probably the same age as me, nineteen, or maybe a bit older.

I can hear my best friend Sarah's words in my head: *You're never gonna lose your v-card if you don't go on any dates.*

She's right. I should say yes. I should at least have coffee with this boy.

He smiles hopefully, and his eyes dart back to my breasts. His tongue flicks over his lips and this time he doesn't bother to look back up at my face.

I should. But there's only one man I'm interested in dating, and it's certainly not this boob-obsessed adolescent.

"Sorry." I give him what I hope is a reluctant smile. "I'm not allowed to date."

His gaze darts up to mine, and his brow furrows in confusion.

It's kind of true. My dad is always joking that I'm not allowed to go out with any boys. He banned me from dating when I was younger, but since I turned eighteen, he has no right to stop me. But the truth is, there's only one man I want to date, and he's not interested in me at all.

"How old are you?" the boy asks.

"I'm nineteen."

He looks concerned. "You should be able to make your own decisions."

He's getting indignant on my behalf, and it's kinda sweet but awkward. I was hoping he'd get the hint without me having to spell it out.

I shrug, which is the wrong move because his wandering eyes lock on my wobbling boobs. Ah, the pleasures of being a curvy girl. Every movement I make takes my boobs a few seconds to catch up.

"My dad's pretty tough. Ex-military, Special Forces."

The boy stands up straight, getting his elbows off my reception desk and his eyes off my tits.

"He doesn't let you date? Can't you go out anyway? You're an adult."

This boy's sweet, and maybe what I'm about to do is a little mean, but I hate saying a flat-out no. Besides, maybe it will scare him away for good and I won't have to put up with his boob staring anymore.

"I went on a date once without him knowing," I lie. "He tracked us down. Broke both the guy's arms."

The boy goes pale, and I try not to smile. "Broke his arms?" he asks faintly.

"Oh, don't worry." I'm really getting into this now. "They reckon he'll be out of hospital in a few more months."

The boy backs away from the reception desk looking horrified.

At that moment, the door that leads through to the office opens, and Leo strides through.

My pulse jumps up a notch at the sight of him. His weathered features and salt-and-pepper hair. The scar that runs behind his ear to halfway down his neck. The tattoos that snake down his thick, muscular arms, telling the story of his life.

Leo's gaze finds mine, a slight smile on his lips that disappears when he sees the boy, who has made the mistake of stealing another look at my chest.

"What the fuck are you staring at?"

Leo strides toward him and the boy stumbles backward, a look of pure terror on his face.

"I was… I was…"

Leo doesn't give him time to explain.

"You keep your eyes on me, kid, or on the floor."

The boy is shaking so hard I think he's going to wet himself.

"I was just bringing her some coffee, that's all. Don't break my arms, please."

Leo pauses and casts a look over his shoulder at me. His eyebrows shoot up in a questioning look.

Leo's blocking the boy's view of me so he can't see me trying not to crack up. I give my shoulders a little shrug, and Leo's eyes glint with mischief.

Then he puts his hard-ass Army face on and turns back to the boy.

"I don't want to see you in here again. If Amy wants a coffee, I'll fetch it for her. You stay the fuck away from her. You understand?"

"Yes, sir." The kid trembles and I kind of feel sorry for him, but then I remember the uncomfortable feeling of his eyes on my boobs and all sympathy vanishes. Besides, I'm too busy enjoying the way Leo's back ripples with tension.

"Now get the fuck out of here."

He takes a step back, giving the kid enough room to scramble out of the door.

When Leo turns around, I burst out laughing. He shakes his head at me as he saunters over to the reception desk.

"Break his arms? What was that all about?"

I tell him about the story I concocted about my dad and how he must have assumed Leo was my father.

Leo grins, and by the time I've finished telling him the

story, we're both laughing so hard my side hurts. I always end up laughing when I'm with Leo. He has a way of making me feel good whenever he's around.

"Good story, kid."

He ruffles my hair, and the good feeling inside me vanishes.

That's all I am to Leo. A kid.

He still thinks of me as a girl. He hasn't noticed that I've grown into a woman.

I've been in love with my father's best friend ever since I was twelve years old.

Dad was back from tour, and him and Mom were arguing again. Only this time, the arguing was quiet, which was worse than the shouting. I heard Mom use the word divorce, and I ran outside, too scared to hear any more.

I ran out to the treehouse and climbed inside. There were some loose boards in the ceiling, and I pulled them aside and pulled myself up onto the roof, hidden by the foliage of the maple tree.

I stayed there until the light faded and didn't come down even when they were calling my name.

It was Leo who found me huddled in the tree, shivering in the cool evening air.

He climbed up and sat with me, taking off his jacket to drape it over my shoulders.

At first neither of us spoke. He just sat with me until the light completely faded from the sky. Then he started telling me jokes. Bad, cheesy jokes, but they made me laugh.

He told me funny stories about my dad on tour, and by

the time another half hour had passed, the scary feeling of not knowing what was happening had gone, and I was in love with my father's best friend.

When we climbed down from the treehouse, when my mom cried with relief and Dad opened his arms, I looked up at Leo, wanting to stay with him, to laugh with him rather than face the reality of what I knew was happening with my parents.

He gave me a reassuring smile. "You're going to be all right, kid." And he ruffled my hair.

Yeah. To him, I'm still that twelve-year-old girl. Will he ever notice that I'm a woman?

2
LEO

It may have been a joke to Amy, chasing away the coffee shop boy this morning, but I was deadly serious. I may not break anyone's arms—although I can't be sure—but I sure as hell won't let any horny young kid get his hands on My Amy.

I think of her as My Amy even though I know it can never be. But goddamn, I am obsessed with my best friend's daughter.

She's always been a great kid, funny and smart. I got protective of her when Tony split with her mom, and that feeling has never left.

Only it's changed over time.

One tour we went away and she was still a girl in pigtails climbing trees. Then we came back and she was a woman, graceful and curvy.

Still funny and smart but in the body of a woman that my eyes can't help following around. Whenever Amy's in the room, I get a few degrees hotter. My pulse races just knowing she's in the building. Since she started working as our receptionist, it's been pure torture.

I'm waiting for my obsession with Amy to pass. It's got too. She's still a goddamn teenager and I'm nearly forty years old. But when I see some young kid trying to hit on her, I see red. The threat to that boy was real.

Amy may be off limits to me, but I won't let any other man touch her.

"Leo." Tony thumps me on the shoulder, his meaty hand making my teeth rattle. "Can I ask a favor?"

"No, Tony, I told you before. I won't hold your willy while you pee."

We're in the kitchen, and the cheap joke gets a laugh from the other guys. Tony just shakes his head as he pulls out the chair next to mine.

He's had a lifetime of my jokes, so he's practically immune.

"I gotta go out of town this weekend and I need a favor."

The chair creaks as he sits down, and I frown, wondering if it'll take his weight. He's big, my best friend. Huge.

That's how we became friends.

I was a small kid for my age, and on the first day of elementary school, another boy stole my schoolbag. A bunch of kids stood in a circle and threw it around between them.

It was a second-hand bag that my mom got from the charity shop, and it had a broken zipper and another kid's name on it that I'd tried to scribble out.

I grew up in a shitty neighborhood, but even by their

standards I was poor. Me and Mom lived in the trailer park in Temptation Bay.

"We don't want white trash in our school," one of the kids taunted.

I stuck my fists up ready for a fight. I might have been poor, but I knew how to defend myself.

"Come here and say that, fuck face."

Yeah, I also learned some pretty choice language in the trailer park.

The whole circle of boys rushed me, and with a roar I ran at the leader, landing him a punch in the nose.

The other boys came at me, and as they took me down, I thrashed blindly, fists and feet connecting with flesh. Then there was an almighty roar, and the biggest kid I'd ever seen started grabbing boys and pulling them off me.

I scrambled to my feet, and we stood side by side, throwing punches like our lives depended on it. We might have been outnumbered but we made up for it in intensity, and together we thrashed our way out of the circle.

The boys ran away, clutching bloody noses and sore stomachs. I could feel warm blood trickling down my face, but I felt elated.

I had beaten the bullies, and I had a friend.

"I'm Tony," the kid said. "You fight good."

I grinned at him, and he grinned back through bloody teeth. Then the teachers came running and we took off.

Tony and I both got suspended from school for a week, and we've been inseparable ever since.

We've been through a lot of shit together, enlisting at the same time, getting into the Special Forces together, and going on countless tours. I'd do anything for Tony.

If he's away for the weekend, he probably needs me to feed his cat or water his tomato plants or something.

"Sure. What do you need?"

"I need you to keep an eye on Amy for me."

Fuck. I keep my expression neutral, hoping he can't detect the turmoil inside me at the mere mention of her name.

"She's going to a music festival." He snorts and shakes his head as if he's just told me she's going to meet the devil. "There'll be drinking there and God knows what else."

Amy moved in with Tony when her mom relocated to LA, and it tortures me every time I go around. But even I can see he's too protective of her.

"She's a sensible kid. I don't think she drinks. You gotta let her have some fun."

"And there'll be boys. It's an overnight festival."

The words freeze the smile on my face. Tony cracks his knuckles, and I feel my anger rising as much as his.

I'm jealous of the teenage boy that will get to touch her creamy thighs, kiss her soft lips, touch her heavy breasts.

My hand forms a fist and I punch my palm under the table.

"Is she going with a boy?"

It comes out strained, but Tony's too preoccupied to notice.

"She's going with a group. Sarah organized it, and there're guys in the group. She says she's not interested in any of them, but she may not be telling me the truth. Although I don't know why she'd lie to me," he adds thoughtfully as he cracks his thick knuckles.

"No, can't think of a reason why she'd lie," I say blithely.

He gives me a sharp look. "Are you trying to be funny?"

I was. She's probably terrified of her father. The story about ripping off a boy's arms may be made up, but it's probably not far from the truth of what Tony would do to anyone who touched his little girl.

The thought sobers me up. If I ever did move on my feelings for Amy, it would be suicide.

"I've got a ticket for the festival." He pulls it out of his pocket. "I was going to go, but something's come up."

He pushes the ticket at me, and I stare at the piece of paper

"Summer DubFest," it says. "You want me to go to a music festival with a bunch of kids?"

"I know it's a lot to ask, man, but anything could happen to her there. She's only nineteen. I don't want to ruin her fun, just make sure she's safe."

Oh man, he is far too protective. Even I know you have to give your kids space, let them leave the nest and all that. But this is My Amy we're talking about. I hate the idea of her hooking up with another man as much as Tony does.

"I'll do it."

Relief floods his face. "You don't have to tell her you're there. No need to cramp her style. Just keep some distance and make sure no one's taking advantage of her. There'll be older people there. She's still so young…"

He trails off and looks away.

I know how hard it was for Tony to leave his family

every time we went on tour. He feels like he missed out on a lot of Amy's life, and now he's trying to make up for it the only way he knows how.

"Caroline thinks I'm being overprotective."

His lips pull together in a thin line. He doesn't talk about his ex-wife much. He'd never say it to me, but I can tell after all these years that it's still painful for him.

"That's why I'm letting her go at all. To prove to Caroline that I'm capable of letting Amy grow up."

"Except you're having her followed?"

Tony grins. "Neither of them needs to know about that part. It's our secret ops mission."

He taps his nose and gives me a wink.

We did a hell of a lot of missions together over the years, but protecting his daughter may be my most important.

I take the ticket out of his hand and pull out the pamphlet it comes with. There's a list of bands I've never heard of. I'll be surrounded by twenty-somethings who are drunk or high and horny. Sounds like my idea of hell.

But I'll do it for my best friend. I'll do it for Amy. If any fucker tries to get close to her, I might just break his fucking arms.

3
AMY

The ground beneath me thumps to the bass of the music. Sweaty bodies sway along to the beat while voices sing out of tune to the popular song.

Sarah's standing in front of me, and she turns to catch my eye, giving me a lazy alcohol-induced smile. She takes my hand, her palm sweaty from the heat of the crowd.

She says something that I can't hear over the music and offers me her water bottle. I'm parched but I learned earlier that it's not water she's got in there. It's pure vodka, and the last thing I want is to get drunk.

I shake my head. She shrugs her shoulders, letting her hand drop mine, and turns back to the stage while taking a sip from the bottle.

One of the boys from our group, Aiden, slaps an arm around Sarah's shoulder and takes the bottle off her. He takes a long swig, upending the contents into his mouth. Then he throws the empty bottle into the air, letting out a loud whoop.

I cringe as the bottle lands somewhere in the crowd of

people, probably hitting someone on the head. But Aidan doesn't care.

He starts dancing to the music with his arms flailing in the sir.

I step back, trying to give him room, and he half turns, stopping mid-move when he catches me looking at him. I drop my eyes quickly before he gets the wrong idea.

Too late.

I feel his eyes on me, roaming over my cut-off shorts and fringed mid-drift top. I borrowed it from Sarah. She wouldn't let me come to the festival in my plain jeans and t-shirt.

I pull the fringe down, trying to cover my stomach, but all that does is make my cleavage pop out at the top.

Aidan gives me a wide-mouthed grin as his eyes travel up my body.

He takes his arm from around Sarah and holds it out to me instead. I try to back away, but he grabs my wrist. His hand is sweaty and covered in dust from the festival.

"Come dance with me."

His breath is alcohol tainted, and with the crowd around us and the loud music, I feel a wave of dizziness.

This is not where I want to be, in a dusty field with a crowd of drunk boys.

I shake my head and pull my hand out of his grasp. Aidan narrows his eyes at me, but before he can grab me again, I put my hand on Sarah's shoulder, making her turn around.

"I need some air."

I shout so that Sarah will hear me. She looks disappointed.

"I don't want to miss the next set."

"It's fine," I say. "I'll be under the trees in our chillout spot."

It's not a big festival, only a few thousand people, and when we first arrived, we spent some time sitting under a copse of trees in the shade. I would have liked to spend the whole day there, watching from afar and away from the main crowd. But everyone else wanted to see the bands up close.

I couldn't care less about the music. It's too loud for me, too bassy, too many people.

As I push through the throng of sweaty bodies, trying to get out of the crowd, the skin on the back of my neck starts to prickle. I've had this feeling ever since I arrived, like someone's watching me.

I glance around quickly, but all I see are groups of smiling people dancing or swaying in a happy daze.

Someone else is moving a few feet behind me, but I can't see them. All I get is a flash of silver hair under a khaki-colored cap.

"You're blocking my view." A woman wearing shorts and a bikini top stands with her hands on her hips and her eyebrows pulled together. I guess not everyone here is in a good mood.

"Sorry," I mumble as I keep going, pushing through groups of people until the crowd gets thinner and the air fresher.

Gulping in large breaths of fresh air, I head for the trees. How I let Sarah talk me into coming here, I have no idea.

I sink into the shade of a large elm and take a few deep

breaths. The air is cooler here, the music a muffled hum rather than so loud that it hurts my ears.

When we first arrived, this shady spot under the trees was packed with people. Now most of the festival goers are in the crowd watching the band on the main stage.

The place is littered with trash, empty bottles and food packets left behind. So much for our generation supposedly caring about the environment.

There are a few groups of people dotted about on the grass. The smell of weed wafts in the air, and tinkles of laughter drift above the sound of the music. A couple is making out on the grass, rolling on top of each other.

"Get a room!" someone yells.

But the couple don't stop their energetic kissing.

I can't believe I let Sarah talk me into this. It's only for one night, but if there was a way to leave right now, then I would.

We're sharing a tent, but something tells me she's going to hook up with one of the guys from the group tonight. Which means sleeping in a tent alone.

My mind wanders to Leo and what he's doing now. Probably something civilized and adult, like having a decent dinner and drinking a beer while watching the Rams play.

I would rather be snuggled on the couch with takeout watching sports than stuck in this field with a bunch of wasted kids.

If Leo could see me know, he'd for sure think I was a still a kid.

"Hey, gorgeous."

I startle at the sound of Aidan's voice. He must have

sneaked up behind me, and now he's leaning against the tree, watching me.

"Aren't you watching the band?" I ask, trying to hide my annoyance. I came here to be alone. The last thing I want is to chat with Aiden.

It's nearly twilight, and the sky is darkening. But I can see the lascivious look on his face, his eyes half-lidded, raking over my body.

Sarah hinted that Aidan would be my type. She's keener for me to lose my v-card than I am. But it certainly isn't going to be to a guy who chugs vodka straight from a bottle.

"I'd rather watch you."

Oh god, he's hitting on me. That's the last thing I want. I scan the grassy slope, hoping to see Sarah or anyone else from the group. But there's no one I recognize. They must all be watching the band still.

Aidan sits next to me, positioning himself too close than what's comfortable, and puts a sweaty hand on my thigh.

"I like you, Anna."

I shift away, pushing his hand off my thigh.

"It's Amy."

Aidan snort laughs. "Amy, Anna…What's in a name?" He's obviously drunk and he lurches at me, sending a waft of liquor my way. "That's Shakespeare, you know? *Hamlet*."

He says it like I should be impressed. But he's got the wrong play.

"*Romeo and Juliet*," I correct him.

"Huh?"

"It's a line from *Romeo and Juliet*."

His eyes narrow, and I realize I've made a mistake. That's another thing about boys. Their fragile egos can't stand being shown up by a woman.

Aiden regards me for a long moment, and I can almost hear his brain processing. Silently, I will him to get up and leave, but instead, his features relax into a grin.

"You're smart too." He runs a slippery hand up my thigh.

I stop his hand with mine.

My mouth is dry, and I feel nauseous. My heart beats rapidly and I'm sure he must hear it. Aiden's a big guy, a football player. It's almost dark, and there aren't a lot of people around. I make my voice steady so he doesn't hear how frightened I am.

"I'm not interested, Aidan." I say it firmly, looking him directly in the eye so there can be no misunderstanding.

I'm about to get up when he grabs me by the shoulders and pushes me to the ground. I'm so taken by surprise that I gasp.

"You don't have to be interested, Amy. Just let me kiss you."

My body freezes in shock. I'm aware of the earth beneath me and the hard press of his body on mine. This can't be happening.

Then his alcohol breath invades my nostrils as his mouth searches for mine. The stench of his breath spurs me into action, and using all my strength, I struggle beneath him.

"Get off me..."

Aiden tries to kiss me but he's slow and drunk. I can't

get out from under him, but I manage to pull my leg up and knee him in the groin. He lets out an angry bark. But it's not enough to get him off.

Then Aiden gives a yelp, and the weight is lifted off me. I roll away from him as he's lifted into the air by someone grabbing him from behind.

I sit up on my elbows, panting, the fear subsiding to relief when I see a large man with Aiden in a hold. It's the man in the khaki hat.

His back's to me as he punches Aidan in the face and sends him sprawling in the dirt.

"She said no, shithead."

Aiden scrambles in the dirt, holding his bloody nose. The man advances on him, and I can only see his back, strong muscles rippling under his t-shirt. His fists are bunched up and angry veins pop in his neck.

He's going to kill him.

The thought jumps into my head, and while I hate Aiden for what he did, I don't want anyone dead.

"Stop." It comes out as a whimper, and the man freezes.

He turns around and I gasp. The man in the khaki hat is Leo.

4
LEO

My vision is blurred with a red mist and an angry tunnel that leads straight to this asshole that thinks it's okay to touch My Amy.

He's crawling away from me on the ground, holding his bloody nose, and I know without a doubt that I will pummel his sorry ass into oblivion for touching a woman without her consent. For touching Amy.

"Stop." Amy's voice slices through the mist, stopping me in my tracks. "You'll kill him."

There's a plea in her voice, and while I'm certain she doesn't have any feelings for this piece of shit, she doesn't want him dead.

Her voice trembles, and I realize that in my haste to kill this bastard, I haven't checked on my girl. It means revealing that I'm here, but I don't give a fuck. Amy's not staying in this shithole for one second longer.

Slowly, I turn around, and she gasps in surprise, her mouth popping open in a perfect O.

"Are you hurt?"

I kneel by her side, my gaze running over her body. If there's any bruise or mark on her, I will track that fucker down and kill him.

Amy stares at me wide-eyed.

"What are you doing here, Leo?"

She's covered in dirt, but otherwise there's no physical damage, which means that asshole just got his life back.

I can't explain to her now about her overprotective father whose instincts were right about this festival. Instead, I slide one arm around Amy's waist and the other under her legs and lift her off the ground.

"I'm taking you home."

She lets out a sob and leans into my chest, her head resting right over my thumping heart.

"Do you need to get anything?"

She shakes her head. "Just get me out of here."

The scumbag has wisely made a run for it because he's nowhere to be seen when I turn around with Amy in my arms.

She leans against me like an exhausted child as I navigate the groups of people dotted about on the grass.

The crowd thins out as we move away from the horrendous music that's been assaulting my ears all day. I head to the security entrance where I know some of the guys, and they open a side gate for us.

With Amy still in my arms, I unlock my car and use one arm to pull the passenger door open. Before I place her into the seat, I look down at the woman in my arms.

Her body is curled into mine, and she's clinging to me around the neck. She looks vulnerable, and a wave of anger courses through me again when I think of that asshole.

"You're okay now, angel. I've got you." I kiss the top of her forehead, breathing in the fragrance of her lavender shampoo.

I slide her into the passenger seat and jog around to my side of the car.

Amy sits silently, her legs curled up in the seat as we drive to my place.

I don't push her. I don't ask her questions. It's enough that I've got her in my car and I'm taking her home where I can look after my girl.

5
AMY

*E*mbarrassment sits in the pit of my stomach. Leo had to rescue me like I was a child. The way he scooped me up in his arms felt good, but it also felt like I was twelve years old again.

The silence sits heavy as we drive to his place, but I'm not ready to talk. I'm not ready to speak about the fact that I can't look after myself and I need my dad's best friend to rescue me because I'm too much of a child to take care of myself.

I have no idea what Leo was doing at the festival, but I'm glad he was there. Just when I needed him the most, Leo turned up like my shining knight.

We pull into his garage and Leo cuts the engine. We sit facing the garage wall in silence.

"You could have taken me home."

In the darkness of the garage, Leo turns to look at me. He's still angry, but there's something else in his expression, something unreadable that sets a tug of longing deep in my core. Could that be desire? Or is he angry and disappointed that I let myself get into a stupid situation?

"I'm not leaving you alone tonight, Amy."

I've been living with Dad ever since Mom took a job in Los Angeles. With him away for the weekend, I'm grateful again for Leo's thoughtfulness. The last thing I want is to be alone tonight.

"What were you doing at the festival?"

It seems strange that Leo was there. I'm sure that Summer DubFest isn't his scene. The serious look drops from Leo's face, and he gives me one of his cheeky grins.

"I love EDM."

I snort laugh because I know he's lying. Leo is a fan of country music, like Dad. They play old records together and argue over which is the better Kenny Rogers album.

"Come on. Let's get you inside."

He opens the car door, putting a stop to that line of questioning. I don't know why Leo was at the festival, but I'm glad he was.

I've been in Leo's house hundreds of times but never without Dad. I stand awkwardly in the kitchen while he makes hot chocolate.

I've got nothing with me but the small purse I always carry over my shoulder. Taking my phone out, I message Sarah to let her know that I've left and ask her to take my stuff home with her tomorrow.

She doesn't reply, which makes me think she probably hasn't even noticed I've gone.

Leo sets the hot chocolate in front of me. Then he holds up a bag of marshmallows.

"One or two?"

Oh great. Marshmallows in hot chocolate is something you'd give a child.

"I'm not a kid anymore, Leo. I drink coffee these days."

He pauses with a marshmallow in his hand.

"You want some coffee before bed?"

He stuffs the marshmallow in his mouth and keeps speaking as he chews.

"I always have two." He pops two marshmallows into his mug. "Don't tell anyone this, but even in the Army, whenever I could get it, I had hot chocolate before bed." He speaks conspiratorially with that dancing look in his eyes, so I can't tell if he's telling the truth or making up a story to make me laugh.

"Really? You drank hot chocolate while on secret missions?" I don't bother to hide the skepticism in my voice.

"Oh yeah, we all did." He pops two marshmallows in the top of my mug. "Your dad liked a warm cup of cocoa while he polished his gun. Kieren laced his with whiskey, and Bronn was the worst. He put the whole unit on parade once because someone only gave him one marshmallow instead of two."

I'm giggling by this point, imagining these hard men drinking warm cocoa.

"You're messing with me."

Leo looks mock offended. "I'm risking my life here telling you a state secret. The entire military would fall apart if we ran out of hot chocolate."

By now I'm laughing and the shame of what happened earlier is slipping away. This I why I love being around Leo. When he's here, nothing ever seems that bad.

"You want a shower? Wash that festival off you?"

I shudder at mention of the festival, and Leo looks concerned.

"Are you okay, Amy? Did that asshole hurt you?"

I do a mental check through my body. There will probably be a bruise on my elbow where he pushed me in the dirt. But other than that, I feel okay.

"No. I'm fine. I got him a good knee in the balls though."

Leo grins. "That's my girl."

I take a sip of hot chocolate, letting the sugary warmth settle into my bones. "Are you ever going to tell me what you were doing at an EDM festival?"

I lick the chocolate off my lips, and his gaze darts to my mouth. When his eyes come back to mine, his expression is deadly serious.

"I was there to protect you, Amy."

The way he says it with his eyes like deep pools of water and his voice deep and raspy makes my insides quiver.

The thought of Leo protecting me is appealing. If only it wasn't like a father protecting a child.

"Do you want a shower? Wash this grime off?"

He touches my arm where it's stained with dirt, and a shock of heat goes through me. He must feel it too because his eyes dart to mine. Our gazes lock, and my pulse quickens.

He's not looking at me like I'm a girl anymore. He's looking at me like he wants me.

A bolt of realization hits my stomach. Leo wants me as much as I want him. The unreadable expression I see on his face sometimes—it's desire.

Feeling emboldened, I bite my lower lip.

"Will you wash it off for me?"

His eyes widen and a groan escapes his lips. The sound rumbles through my body, sending a wet heat to my panties.

"Amy..." He drops my arm and turns away, running a hand through his hair.

Panic races through me. I've fucked up. I've read him wrong, and now I've embarrassed myself even more.

"Just joking..." I give a casual laugh that sounds as forced as it feels.

Leo doesn't turn around, and I watch his back heave up and down as he breathes deeply.

"You can sleep in the spare room tonight, Amy. And tomorrow I'll drop you back home. I'll get you a towel."

Without turning around, Leo heads up the stairs. I follow, feeling like a big fuck-up.

Every instinct is telling me that he wants me, but his actions are showing the opposite. I have no experience with men. I don't know how to seduce him or if that's even what he wants.

I follow Leo's rigid back up the stairs and down the hallway. He stops by a cupboard to give me a towel.

"I'll see you in the morning."

Leo doesn't look me in the eye, and I watch him go down the hall and through a door at the end that must be his bedroom.

I've never seen Leo act so serious. I've never known him not to turn an awkward situation into a joke.

As his door clicks shut, I make a decision. This is the opportunity I've been waiting for. I've got Leo alone for a night. It's my chance to prove to him that I'm not a little girl anymore. I'm going to show him that I'm a woman.

6
LEO

My breathing comes in shallow ragged breaths as I lean against the door of my bedroom trying not to think about Amy soaping herself down in the shower.

I dig my knuckles into my palm, needing to take some of the heat out of my throbbing cock before I stride down the hall and pummel her virgin pussy.

Every fiber of my body is straining against my mind, telling me to go claim my woman. It takes all the restraint I have to listen to that part of my brain that's still talking reason.

I've wanted Amy for so long, but I can't have her. I can't do that to Tony.

He trusted me to look after his daughter, not fuck her.

My cock's sticking straight out of my pants, my body telling me that I should be in the shower with her right now soaping down her soft body. Damn, just thinking about her in my shower has me practically coming in my pants.

My cock throbs as I pull it out of my boxers, needing some relief. It only takes two stokes while thinking about Amy's soapy hand running over her perfect tits before I shoot into my hand with a dissatisfied grunt.

Panting against the door, I feel no relief.

I don't think I'll sleep knowing Amy's down the hall. But at least she's safe here. I may not be able to have her, but no other fucker will.

I wash up in the bathroom and strip to my boxers before climbing in between the sheets.

I'm sitting up in bed watching a video on my phone when there's a timid knock at the door. It opens and Amy appears in the doorway wearing nothing but a bath towel wrapped around her body.

The blood instantly pulses to my dick as I take in her bare shoulders, her slick thighs, droplets of water catching on her skin.

"I, um, don't have anything clean to wear."

It takes me a moment to realize she's spoken. I'm too busy watching a droplet of water as it snakes between her cleavage. I tear my eyes away and shuffle out of bed sideways, trying to hide my boner, but her eyes dart to it anyway. They widen when she sees the tent in my boxers, and I cover it with a pillow, doing a silly sideways crab walk to my drawers.

Because that's what I do. I make jokes when I don't know how to deal with the situation, and dealing with your best friend's daughter giving you an aching boner for the second time in a night is about as awkward as it gets.

"You can borrow a t-shirt."

I fling an old t-shirt at her, and she slides it over her head, letting the towel drop to the floor.

The t-shirt comes up just above her thighs, and I know she's not wearing underwear underneath, which does nothing to ease the ache in my balls.

"Thanks."

She turns slowly to the door, and I get a glimpse of butt cheek as the t-shirt rides up. A perfect round peach just waiting to be squeezed.

A groan escapes me, and I turn it into a cough.

Amy looks around and bites her lower lip.

"I don't want to sleep alone tonight. Can I sleep in here with you?"

She looks up at me through lowered lashes and I get the feeling she's trying to seduce me, but she also looks vulnerable and uncertain, reminding me of how young and innocent she is.

"Amy, I don't think that's a good idea."

My voice comes out croaky because my throat's dry and I'm having a hard time swallowing. My eyes are fixed on her body, on where the white t-shirt is sticking to her wet breasts, showing pale skin through the thin fabric.

Her eyes darken with mischief, and she looks down at the pillow I'm holding over my crotch.

"Or maybe it's the best idea." She moves toward the bed, and I watch, fascinated by her confidence as much as her body. "I'm not a child anymore, Leo."

As she says it, she kneels on the bed, crawling on her hands and knees over to where I'm desperately trying to cover the huge boner that's dripping pre-cum all over my boxers.

"Amy..."

It comes out as a rasp because I'm mesmerized by her. The sultry look she's giving me is what my fantasies have been about for the past several months, ever since she grew those gorgeous breasts.

"Let me show you that I'm a woman."

She creeps further forward, and I back away from the bed until I run into the dresser on the other side of the room. She's my best friend's daughter. I can't do this. No matter how much my body aches for her.

"I have no doubt you're a woman, Amy. But I won't take advantage of you like this."

She sits back on her haunches and the t-shirt rides up her thighs, giving me a glimpse of springy black hair.

"You won't be taking advantage. I want you, Leo. I've always wanted you. Don't you know that?"

She looks frustrated and vulnerable, and something clicks inside me. The laughing together, the looks we share—I thought it was one-sided, my obsession with Amy. But I realize she feels it too.

Amy wants me. She has feelings for me as strong as the feelings I have for her.

"I've been trying to get your attention, but you only ever see me as a kid. I'm not a kid anymore, Leo. I'm a woman."

As she says it, she pulls the t-shirt over her head and tosses it off the bed. Her breasts hang soft and heavy, with large dark circles around the peaky nipples.

My mouth waters, my dick throbs, my chest is heavy, and it's hard to breathe.

I've never wanted another woman the way that I want

Amy, and here she is, naked on my bed. If it was any other woman, I'd already be inside her. But she's not just any woman. She's my best friend's daughter and completely forbidden to me.

"I can't do this, Amy…"

I should look away. I should cover her up and leave the room. But I'm mesmerized by her silky breasts and the challenging look she's giving me.

"You don't have to do anything, Leo."

As she says it, her hand slides over her breasts, finding a dark nipple. She tweaks it in her fingers and a shudder goes through her as the nipple pebbles.

"Amy…" My voice has a warning note to it. I can't let this happen. Tony would kill me if I debased his daughter.

I grit my teeth and pull on all the military discipline I can muster. "I won't take advantage of you."

"You're not taking advantage of me." She slides her other hand over her thick thighs and into the space between her legs. "You're not doing anything to me."

Technically she's correct. It doesn't ease my conscience, but I can't look away as Amy parts her thighs and strokes her palm over her glistening folds. Her pussy lips peek out from between her fingers, pink and glistening and so fucking tempting.

"I always think about you when I touch myself."

Her voice is breathy as she strokes herself, one hand working her pussy and the other tugging at her nipples. My cock jerks against the pillow, and I slide my hand into my boxers, finally giving in to the aching need of my body. Her eyes smile in triumph as she sees me give a long tug to my cock.

"I imagine it's you rubbing your cock against my pussy."

The dirty words coming from her innocent mouth send a bolt of pleasure to my cock and a groan from my lips.

"Fuuck, Amy…"

"Do you think of me, Leo? Do you think of me when you're touching yourself?"

"Baby, you have no idea."

My mind goes to the things I've imagined doing to Amy. Amy on her knees, Amy on her back, Amy up against the wall as I plunge into her. But nothing compares to this moment, to Amy on my bed, pleasuring herself.

Her chest heaves and her breath comes out in shallow gasps as her palm works herself into a frenzy.

"I imagine it's your hands on me, Leo. You touching me. Only you."

Her head drops back and her eyes close as she gets close to climax.

"I'll be the only one to touch you," I growl. "You're mine, Amy. Only mine."

Because there's no going back from this moment. We've crossed a line. I haven't touched her. I haven't disrespected my friend. But there is no way I'm letting Amy go now. Whatever it takes, Amy will be mine.

"Yes," she gasps, "I'm yours, Leo."

She shudders as she says my name. Her mouth drops open and she cries out, her palm pushing into her center as she comes.

"Mine," I gasp as hot cum shoots into my palm. My cock spasms as I watch her body tremble with pleasure.

I don't know how I'm going to square this with Tony, and I don't care. Amy is mine, and I'm not letting her go.

7
AMY

My body trembles in relief as the orgasm races through me. Leo shudders and groans, and as he comes in his hand, a deep satisfaction rolls through me.

If he had any doubts that I am a woman, they must be gone by now. I've shown him my body is all woman.

He must see how we can be together now. Unless I've tempted him too far and it's not what he wants.

Panic grips at my stomach. Then I remember the words he said to me.

You're mine, Amy. Only mine.

My body relaxes. He wants this as much as I do.

Leo's wiping his hand on a tissue, and I suddenly feel awkward, shy at my nakedness, which doesn't make sense considering how bold I was a few moments ago. But no man's ever seen me naked before.

I sit back on the bed and grab the t-shirt, ready to pull it over my head.

"Leave it." Leo grabs the t-shirt and snatches it out of my hand. "I want you to sleep naked."

The words send a tingle through me, and my pussy convulses. Leo pulls a tissue from a box by the bed and hands it to me.

"I won't sleep with you until I've spoken to Tony." At the mention of my father, an uneasy feeling pierces the happiness. "I won't disrespect my best friend like that."

"I'm an adult, Leo. I can make my own decisions.

I stick out my lower lip. I've just been given this new plaything and he wants to take it away.

"Don't look at me like that, angel." He pulls down the top of the duvet and pats the bed, inviting me in.

"You're mine, Amy. And I will claim that sweet pussy. But there's a right way to do this, and that's what we're going to do."

I climb into bed, and he slides in next to me, his front to my back. His arms go around my body, and it feels so right to be in his arms that I let out an involuntary sigh.

Something hard presses into my back, and I give a gasp when I realize what it is. I didn't realize men could get hard again so soon.

Leo chuckles at my reaction. His fingertips slide down my arm, making my skin tingle and my pussy light up with heat.

"I thought you didn't want to have sex?"

His lips press against my neck, making the last part of my sentence climb up an octave.

"We're not having sex. But it doesn't mean we can't do what we just did again."

I press my hips against him and slide my hand back

and over his thighs. Because I want more. I want all of him.

Leo stops my hand and places it in front of me between my thighs. He turns my palm around so it's pressed against my pussy. I feel a wave of disappointment. I haven't yet broken down his defenses. He doesn't want me enough to give in to temptation.

"Touch yourself, Amy. Show me you're a woman."

His words are breathy and delicious, and I close my eyes and float away as pleasure courses through my body.

I may not have all of Leo, but I'm in his bed and that's enough for now.

The sun's already peeping through the windows by the time I wake up the next morning. The sheets feel slick on my naked body, and I stretch lazily, remembering what happened last night.

Leo wants me. He's as into me as I am into him.

There's a big smile on my face as I roll over. It disappears when I see the empty side of the bed. My hand reaches out, but the sheets are cold.

Slipping on the oversized t-shirt Leo lent me last night, I pad out of the bedroom and downstairs.

The smell of frying bacon hits me before I reach the kitchen. Leo's humming as he turns the bacon with a dishcloth thrown over his shoulder.

He's wearing old sweatpants that hang off his hips and a tank top that shows off the muscles rippling underneath.

My mouth waters at the sight of him, and my pussy

pulses remembering the way he watched me last night as I touched myself.

"Good morning, beautiful." he says when he sees me.

I could get used to this, waking up to this man every morning.

"You want one egg or two?"

"Two, please." I take a seat on the kitchen stool and watch him as he cooks.

I don't know if the things he said to me last night were spur of the moment or if he really meant them. And I can't tell from the way he's acting.

Leo seems happy, humming to himself as he cracks eggs into the frying pan. But this is what Leo's always like. He's always in a good mood, always humming.

He's so different from my grumpy dad. I don't know how they're such good friends sometimes. The thought of Dad causes a nagging feeling in the back of my brain. He's going to flip when he finds out about me and Leo.

I push the feeling back. I don't want to think about that right now. I only want to think about Leo and the way his butt moves as he shimmies in time to the music he's humming.

A few minutes later, Leo puts a plate of fried eggs and bacon in front of me and slides onto the other kitchen stool.

"What are you up to today?"

My face falls. He's kicking me out. Last night meant nothing. Maybe that's how men and woman interact. They have a sexual encounter and that's it. Maybe I am just a kid playing an adult's game.

"Um, I was supposed to be at that festival."

"Good. I want you all to myself today."

The words make my chest feel light, and the doubts flee my mind.

"Did you mean what you said to me last night?"

Leo puts down his fork, his expression going serious. "Every word."

He puts his hand over mine. "You're mine now, Amy. I need to square it away with Tony, but leave that to me."

I hate talking about my father with Leo, but it seems so important to him.

"You don't think he'll approve?"

Leo barks out a laugh. "He'll hit the roof."

"But you're his best friend. He should trust you with me."

"Exactly. He thought he could trust me with you. And I've taken advantage."

Leo frowns and takes his hand off mine. I see the doubt darken his expression, and I don't like where this is going.

"You didn't take advantage of me." I slip off the stool so I'm standing before him. "You rescued me, and you've been kind to me and…" My hand slides up his thigh and Leo shudders.

His eyes flicker closed, and he draws in a ragged breath. I love how I can make him lose control.

Then his eyes snap open, and his hand stops mine before it reaches the bulge in his pants.

"Do not temp me you, little minx." His eyes are dancing like it's a joke, but I can see the restraint, what it takes him to stop me.

I long to push him over the edge, to make him lose control.

"We're going to spend the day together. Do something fun," he says as he places my hand firmly back on the table.

"I know something fun we could do." I look at him through lowered lashes, loving the way he finds me so tempting.

"Don't push me, Amy."

His voice has a sharp edge to it, and I can tell he's close to breaking. I could keep pushing, but I also like the fact that he wants to do the right thing.

Reluctantly, I pull my gaze away from him and turn on my stool.

"We'll stop by your house to get you some clothes." My t-shirt rides up the back of my bare legs, and he slaps my ass playfully. A spasm of pleasure goes through my body.

"You can't go around with a bare ass all day."

I giggle, loving the way Leo always brings it back to something playful.

I know he's trying to do the right thing so that Dad doesn't kill him, but it's killing me in the process. I want him to touch me, to possess me, to make me his properly.

8
LEO

My balls are aching with the heavy load of cum that's been building all day. Just having Amy by my side is enough to get my dick in a permanent semi.

We spent the day in one of my favorite bays along the coast. You can only get there by walking around the cliffs, which means it's free of tourists.

We swam in the cool ocean and looked for crabs in the rock pools. We lied on a picnic blanket, laughing and talking. I tried to keep my hands off Amy, but it was fucking hard.

I've had a permanent boner ever since I saw her coming out of the ocean in her two-piece, flaunting her curves with the same self-confidence she showed in the bedroom last night.

She wants to prove to me she's a woman, I have no doubt. She's got more confidence than most women twice her age.

Tomorrow I'll speak with Tony. I don't know how it's going to go, but I can guess.

He's not going to be happy that someone wants to be with his little girl, least of all me. He'll probably feel betrayed and taken for a fool. I need to make him see the truth, that I love Amy. That I'll take care of her and that I'll always do right by her.

There is a risk Tony will break my arms, or worse. But I'll take that risk for My Amy. The challenge I face tonight is getting through the night with her virginity intact.

I owe that to my best friend. I won't ravish his daughter until I have his blessing. I need him to know that's not what I'm after from Amy. I'm here for the long haul. I'm here for her. Forever.

Now we're back at my place, and I'm cooking up steamed fish with grilled vegetables while Amy watches me from her perch on the kitchen stool.

"Where did you learn to cook?"

I slide the fish out of the pan and onto the plate, adding a squeeze of lemon and some parsley for garnish.

I learned to cook out of necessity because Mom often wasn't around and I didn't like eating cereal for dinner. But I'm not going to tell Amy my whole story right now. My hard upbringing gave me resilience and fortitude and prepared me for life in the military.

"I've always cooked. Learned as a kid."

I put the plate in front of her and watch as she takes a bite of the buttery potatoes. Her eyes close, and she tilts her head back. Fuck me. Even that movement has my cock throbbing.

"It's good."

"Get used to it because when you move in here, I'll cook for you every night if you like."

Her eyes widen and she almost chokes on her mouthful.

"You want me to move in?"

"I told you, kiddo. I'm crazy about you. You're mine now, and that means waking up next to you every day of my life."

Her face lights up in a beatific smile, making my heart melt like the butter on the potatoes.

"I'll go get my things."

She pretends to slide off the stool, making me laugh.

I laugh a lot when I'm with Amy. Sure, I laugh a lot anyway. Life is for enjoying, after all, but it's even more so when I've got Amy by my side. Everything seems lighter when she's around.

We eat dinner while talking easily and wash the dishes together. And it's so natural, having her by my side and in my house. I can't wait for her to move in permanently.

I'm putting the last of the dishes away when I accidentally brush up against Amy. I've been careful to keep my hands to myself all evening because I know I won't be able to stop myself.

But as my hip brushes hers, the heat coming off her body burns my veins and sends the blood rushing south. I turn away, trying to hide my hard-on, but it's too late.

Amy's gaze locks on the tent in my pants, and she raises an eyebrow at me.

"You must really love doing the dishes."

"Only when it's with you. I don't usually get turned on

by my dinner plates." She laughs, a deep throaty sound that does nothing to help the aching in my loins.

"They are exceptionally nice dinner plates." She puts the last one in the cupboard, and when she turns back to me, she's biting her lower lip.

Her gaze dips to the boner pressing against my jeans, and a mischievous look dances in her eyes.

"Amy…" I give her a warning as she advances toward me because I swear if that woman lays one soft hand on me, I'm done for.

Her teeth sink into her lower lip as her mouth curls up at the edges. Her hand reaches for my jeans, and I don't pull away. I can't pull away.

Her hands caress me through the tough fabric, and the pressure of her palm combined with her lavender scent makes me dizzy.

"We're not doing this, Amy. Not yet."

"I'm not doing anything," she says innocently even as her hands undo my belt buckle.

I want nothing more than to sink into her virgin pussy, but I'm not going to do that until I've spoken with Tony.

With all the restraint and discipline that twenty years in the military has taught me, I put my hand over hers.

"I'm not sleeping with you, Amy. Not yet."

Her thumb sneaks out from under my hand and slowly strokes me through my jeans.

"Who said anything about sleeping together?"

With her eyes locked on mine, she sinks to her knees. I let out a groan when I realize what she wants to do. And help me, God. When she fumbles with my zipper, I don't resist.

"We shouldn't be doing this," I mutter feebly as she slides my jeans off my hips and frees my cock from my sticky boxers.

"I want to make you feel good, Leo."

The words make me groan. My girl on her hands and knees wanting to please me is almost more than I can take.

Her tongue darts out and licks the tip of my cock. "Is this good?"

She looks uncertain, and that innocence almost undoes me.

"You ever done this before?"

There's only one right answer, and it's the one Amy gives when she shakes her head slightly.

"You're my first everything, Leo. My first and only."

Damn right I am.

I'm the first dick she's had in her mouth. I can tell by the way she holds me, uncertain with her mouth clumsily closing over my length. Her inexperience makes it all the more erotic.

Instinctually, she knows how to lick and suck right where I need it. I can't imagine how good she'll be with a little practice.

But I do know we shouldn't be doing this. It's not sex, but it may as well be.

"We should stop, Amy."

But even as I say the words to her, I thrust into her mouth, wanting her to take all of me.

I shouldn't. She's forbidden to me. Out of bounds. But her hot wet mouth around my shaft is too good to resist.

"Amy, stop…"

I'm panting as I say it, breathless and tortured. I want her so bad, but I know I shouldn't.

She looks up at me and runs a hand over her top, pulling down her t-shirt to caress her breasts.

Her mouth turns up at the corners as she sucks me long and hard, tugging at my cock like I'm a stick of candy.

I should stop. I've been trained for resilience, to be disciplined.

My hand goes to her head to pull her off my cock, but her mouth clamps around me.

"We can't do this…"

My words turn into a groan as she opens her throat, taking me all the way into her mouth. She gags on my cock and her eyes widen. I start to pull out, but her hand firmly clamps around me.

No matter what I do, she's not stopping, and it feels so fucking fantastic.

I feel the moment my will breaks. Twenty years of military discipline crumbles in Amy's soft mouth.

My hands fist her hair, and I thrust into her, giving in to my need.

"We shouldn't…" I say feebly. Knowing it's forbidden spurs me on.

Amy's hand slides down to her leggings, and she slips her hand into them, caressing herself as she takes me into her mouth.

I pull her head toward me, pulling her mouth down

my shaft. "You're forbidden…" I say even as I plunge myself into her, pulling her roughly up and down my cock, needing this release so badly.

She gives little yelps of pleasure as I fuck her mouth, her hands working in her pants to bring her to a peak.

My balls pull up tight, and I know I'm about to explode.

"I'm going to cum." I give her a warning and try to pull out, but she clamps onto my cock and sucks for all she's worth.

"I. Shouldn't. Be. Fucking. Your. Mouth." I say the words with every thrust. On the last word, I explode inside her, shooting hot cum to the back of her throat, making her gag and sending my seed dribbling out the sides of her mouth.

Her body tenses and she cries out, coming as she tries to swallow my seed down, her cries tugging on my cock and milking the last drops out of me.

"Fuuck," I groan as I slide myself out of her. I lift her up off the floor and hug her close to me, my thumping heart pressed against her chest.

"Did I do okay?"

She looks anxious, and I kiss her forehead.

"Baby, you did more than okay. You're amazing, and I'm a lucky son of a bitch."

She smiles warmly at my praise.

Her eyelids are drooping, and I can see the day has worn her out. Holding her hand, I lead her upstairs, hoping like hell we can make it through the night with her virginity still intact.

9
LEO

I wake the next morning with the soft curves of Amy pressed to my side. I've got one arm flung over her protectively and an instant hard-on.

I need to speak to Tony today, or else my balls are going to explode.

Amy's still asleep and I snuggle into her neck, breathing in her soft scent.

The doorbell goes, and careful not to disturb my sleeping angel, I slip out of bed. An urgent knock follows the bell, and Amy stirs as I pull on my jeans and a t-shirt.

The banging gets more persistent as I head downstairs.

"All right, keep your hair on," I say as I pull open the door.

Tony's standing there with his fist raised to the door and his brow knitted together. I'd usually turn what I said about keeping your hair on into a joke about Tony's bald head, but not today. Knowing his daughter is naked in my bed upstairs makes my stomach drop into my toes.

"You seen Amy?" Tony pushes past me into the house like he's done a hundred times before. We're best mates. We come and go in each other's homes and don't wait for pleasantries. "She's not at home."

He runs his hand over his head. The hair may be gone, but the habit of pulling at it when he's anxious remains.

"Was she okay at the festival? Did anything happen?"

The festival seems like a lifetime ago. I think back to rescuing her from the horny teenager, but that's nothing compared to what I've been doing to his daughter since.

"She's fine," I manage, not sure how to go on. "I didn't think you were getting back 'til this afternoon."

"I got back early."

Tony's a man of few words. He's been mysterious about where he was going this weekend, and I don't push it. If I had to guess, he's been to help his ex-wife.

He's never gotten over Caroline, Amy's mom, and lately he's been paying her a lot of attention. By the worn look on his face, I'm not sure this weekend went as he'd hoped.

Tony's eyes sweep around the room, and they land on Amy's bag. At the same moment, there's a creak on the stairs and Amy appears in the doorway.

Her hair is messy from sleep, and she's wearing my oversized t-shirt. I hope like hell she's got underwear on underneath.

Tony looks relieved to see her.

"You're here. Thank God."

Amy's eyes widen at the sight of her dad, and she darts a terrified look at me. Tony notices the look and his eyes narrow, trying to figure out what it means.

He's a smart guy, my best friend, and I see the moment he puts two and two together.

The relieved look turns to confusion.

"What the fuck is going on here?" He turns on me. "She better have been sleeping in your spare room, Leo."

I hold my hands up, trying to placate him, my heart hammering in my chest. This isn't how I wanted to tell Tony about us. I imagined sitting him down over a beer and having a man-to-man talk.

But now the moment is happening. I can't back out.

"There's no easy way to tell you this. But Amy and I are together."

Tony blinks at me, trying to process my words, the disbelief turning slowly to fury.

"What do you mean *together*?"

His voice is low and growly, and I've heard him use that same voice just before he's knocked someone unconscious.

"I mean, I love your daughter and I'm going to look after her now."

"Like fuck you are."

The slow growl has turned into a dangerous fury. This isn't good. This is fucking frightening.

"You been messing around with my little girl?"

Tony advances on me, and even though he's at least a foot taller and fucking huge, I clench my jaw and don't back down.

"It's not like that," I say with a calmness I don't feel.

"The fuck it's not. I trusted you, Leo, with my most precious possession, and this is what you do?"

He raises his fist, and I don't dodge the punch. It hits

me directly on the left eye, and pain explodes in my skull. I stagger backwards, collapsing to the floor.

Amy screams and then she's on her dad, trying to pull him off me as he lands another punch.

I don't fight back. I deserve this. No matter how much I love Amy, it was a shitty way to go about things.

"Stop!" Amy screams.

"You fucked my little girl."

Tony throws another punch, but this time I move my head out the way and his fist connects with the wall, leaving a hole in the plaster. I'll have to get that repaired some time, but for now, I don't care. Let him take out his anger on me.

"I'm not a little girl anymore." Amy pulls at Tony's arms, slowing him down. "And I'm still a virgin."

Tony pauses, breathing hard, his narrow eyes locked on mine.

"Leo has been nothing but a gentleman," she continues.

I think about fucking Amy's mouth after dinner last night and know there was nothing gentlemanly about it. But I'll keep that one to myself.

"I love him, Daddy. I love him, and I want to be with him."

Amy is sobbing now, and the sight of her crying makes my heart bleed. It seems to calm Tony, and he turns away from me to put a beefy arm around her shoulders.

"Is that true sweetheart? You love him?"

"Yes," she sobs.

Tony sits back on his haunches, breathing hard. Amy rushes to me, her cool fingers running gently over my face that's already starting to swell.

As Tony watches us together, I see the conflict that's going on inside of him.

"I need to talk to Leo alone."

Amy puts a hand firmly on his shoulder. "Promise you're not going to hit him anymore."

Tony cracks his knuckles, sending a sprinkling of plaster dust into the air.

"Promise, Daddy."

"Okay, okay."

I get off the floor and follow Tony outside. We sit on the bench on my front porch, and he leans forward, his meaty arms resting on his thighs.

"How long?" he asks.

"I've loved Amy since the last time we came back from tour. But I never would have made a move. It was only this weekend when I found out she had feelings for me that I told her how I feel."

Tony doesn't say anything for a long time. My head throbs, and I long to be in Amy's soothing arms, but I need to give him all the time he needs.

"She's only a kid, Leo."

"She's nineteen, Tony. You were married and had Caroline pregnant by that age."

He runs a hand over his bald head. "Yeah, and look how that turned out."

Tony's broken marriage is a sore point. His biggest regret is not making it work with Caroline.

"But I'm not in the military now. I can be there for her. I'll provide for her, look after her. I love her, Tony."

I take a deep breath, not knowing how my next words will go down.

"And I want to marry her."

Tony looks at me sharply. "You really that serious?"

"I've never been more serious in my life. Since we came back last time, I haven't been with another woman. I tried to get Amy out of my head. I knew I shouldn't have these feelings, but the fact is I love her. And I'll love her for the rest of my days."

Tony looks out to the garden and lets out a slow breath.

"I love her more than anything in the world, Leo. You won't know that kind of love until you have kids of your own."

"Fuck." He runs a hand over his head again. "You'll have my fucking grandkids." He snorts and shakes his head. But I feel him relax. I feel his acceptance.

"If anyone can look after her, you can Leo."

"So, we have your blessing?"

He looks at me coolly. "What would you do if I said no?"

I keep my gaze even because he has to know that we'll be together no matter what. "We'll move in together anyway."

"Fuck."

Tony stands up slowly. "I need to get out of here. This is a lot to process." He takes the steps two at a time and turns around on the bottom step. "Leo, you break my little girl's heart, and I will kill you."

I have no doubt he means it. But I also have no doubt that I will cherish Amy for the rest of my days.

10
AMY

I'm watching through the kitchen window, trying to hear what Leo and Dad are talking about. There's been no more fighting, which has to be positive, right?

Dad stands up and walks away, and a few moments later, Leo comes back in the door.

I'm clutching my throat, anxious about what he's going to say.

"Well?"

The skin around Leo's eye is already starting to swell and turn purple, and there's blood coming out of his nose.

He holds up his arms in a wide shrug with a lopsided grin on his face. "Well, he didn't break my arms."

The anxiousness subsides. That's about as much of a blessing as we're going to get from my dad, so I'll take it.

I run into Leo's arms, and he encloses them around me.

"He'll get used to the idea," Leo says.

I pull my head back to look at the purple bruising

that's starting to form around his eye.

"I need to get something on that." I try to pull away, but Leo tightens his arms around me.

"It can wait." Something hard pushes into my belly as I squirm against him. "But this can't." Leo presses his hardness against me, and realization sets in.

"You mean, we can…?"

I suddenly feel shy, which is silly after everything we've done this weekend. But this feels bigger. This feels like it really means something.

"Yes, angel." Leo plants soft kisses on the top of my head. "I'm going to claim you now."

The possessiveness of the statement, the confidence of it sends a thrilling shiver through me. I wiggle my hips against his, deliberately bumping up against his hard-on.

Leo slides a hand smoothly under the t-shirt so he's gripping my buttocks. His hand slides into my panties and he cups my butt cheeks in his hand.

I tilt my head back as his lips move slowly down my neck.

His finger parts my cheeks, and his thumb grazes my back entrance.

I give a gasp of surprise as a tendril of pleasure slices through me. I didn't know being touched there could feel so nice.

Leo chuckles as if reading my mind. "Yes, angel. We've got a lot of exploring to do."

His thumb flutters over my back entrance, and I mewl in pleasure.

"You really like that don't you?"

Leo's voice is tinged with wonder, and I love that we

can explore each other together. I also love the sensations his thumb is making, causing my body to come alive, all my nerve endings waking up.

"I guess so. It's all new to me."

Leo pushes me up against the wall and yanks my panties down. "Let me show you something else."

He crouches before me, and before I have time to worry about what he's doing, his mouth closes over my pussy.

I give a sigh of content as his hot breath shimmers over my folds.

He hoists one leg up over his shoulder, opening my legs to him. It feels vulnerable, but I feel completely safe in Leo's hands. I open my body, leaning back on the wall and letting him explore my most sacred places with his tongue.

One hand slides around my buttocks, and while he licks my front channel, his finger tickles my back entrance. The fluttery sensations cause ripples of pleasure to go through my body. I grab his hair, wanting to pull him into me.

It feels dirty. It feels right. It feels too good to stand. My back arches, my pussy clenches, and without warning, an orgasm rips through me, making both my entrances pulse with pleasure.

Leo keeps the pressure on until my trembling stops. When he slowly sits up, his eyes are hooded, dark with desire.

I'm panting, my cheeks aflame with the embarrassment of what we've just done.

"Is that…normal?"

He pulls me toward him, tucking his fingers under my chin and turning my face up to his.

"Normal is whatever we make it."

My embarrassment subsides, and a feeling of safeness washes over me. This is where I belong. This is the man who will take care of me.

"Come on." Leo takes my hand and leads me toward the stairs. "I want our first time be in a bed."

By the time we make it to his room, the anxious ball in my stomach is churning again. Leo seems to sense it because he starts slow, kissing me softly on the neck and throat, peeling off our clothes slowly until our naked bodies press together on the bed.

His hands never stop moving, caressing, and squeezing, teasing my body until I feel like a ball of putty in his hands—his to do with as he pleases.

Leo kneels before me, his hard cock in his hand, running the shaft over my swollen pussy lips.

"Are you ready, Amy?"

I bite my lower lip and nod. "I'm ready." As I say it, I let my knees fall open, giving him access to the inner most part of me.

Leo takes a sharp intake of breath. "You're beautiful, Amy. So beautiful."

With a slow thrust, he pushes into me. It's tight, so tight, and I feel stretched. My face screws up and my body tenses.

"Open your eyes, Amy, and look at me."

I didn't even realize that I'd closed them until Leo says it.

When I open my eyes, he's staring at me intensely.

"Keep looking at me, angel. I've got you."

Trusting him utterly, I let my body relax. When I do, Leo thrusts in further. I feel something inside of me give and a piercing pain that lasts only an instant. Then it's gone, and all I feel is full, so full of the man I love.

"I love you, Amy."

As he says the words, he pulls out and thrusts in again, making my back arch with pleasure.

"I love you too."

In that moment, I give myself utterly to Leo—heart, body, and soul.

My gaze stays on him as Leo moves slowly in and out, finding the rhythm of our love.

Our bodies press together, and my legs wrap around him. Our bodies become slick with sweat, mingling together as we cry out as one, climbing together toward an impossible peak.

When I think the pressure is too much to bear, it breaks, and waves of ecstasy cascade through me. Leo gives a final jerk, and I feel his hot cum launch into my body.

His hips grind into mine and I wrap my legs tighter, clinging to him with everything that I have.

It's a moment of pure ecstasy, pure contentment, sharing this wonderful feeling with the man I love.

Leo slowly peels out of me, and we lie together, our bodies wrapped in each other. I fit against him perfectly, my soft body against his hard one.

A warm feeling of contentment washes over me. Leo is the only man for me, and I'm exactly where I belong—in his arms.

EPILOGUE

LEO

Three years later…

Early morning sunlight pushes through the autumn leaves of the large maple trees that line our street. Mia shifts in the baby sling, and I wrap a hand around the front of it, giving her a soothing rub and silently praying that she doesn't wake up.

Stifling a yawn, I hum to myself as we continue around the block for the third time this morning.

Hardly anyone else is out at this time of the morning, only a few joggers and dog walkers. Despite the lack of sleep, I wouldn't have it any other way.

I love these early morning walks with my baby girl. It gives Amy a chance to get some sleep, and I get to go out and enjoy the fresh morning air.

A large figure is jogging toward us, and I hold up a hand in greeting as I recognize Tony. He slows down when he reaches us, but I keep walking.

"Sorry, man. If I stop, she'll wake up."

He falls into step with us, a warm look on his face as her peers at his granddaughter.

"How's my girl doing?"

He wiggles his finger at Mia, his voice going all gooey. In all the year's I've known Tony, I've never seen him like this.

He's crazy about his granddaughter, the tough man having been brought to his knees by this tiny human.

"She's good. Still not sleeping through." I envy those parents whose babies sleep through the night at just a few weeks old. Our little girl still can't manage more than about four hours at a time.

I stifle a yawn and Tony chuckles.

"You look rough, man."

"Thanks."

I know he's right. There's more gray hair than there was three months ago, dark smudges permanently under my eyes, and I'm already getting a soft dad bod. If it wasn't for these morning walks, I wouldn't get any exercise.

Tony slaps me on the back. "Rather you than me, man."

He's got the smug look of a man who wisely had his children when he was young and had the energy for it.

"Gotta go. I'll stop by later if you two want a break."

"Appreciate that, man."

Tony jogs off, and I watch him go before turning onto our street.

I quietly let myself into the house, feeling like a ninja when Mia doesn't wake up.

I tiptoe upstairs and poke my head around the bedroom door.

Amy's sprawled out on the bed, her hair fanned across the pillow and her mouth dropped open. Her hair's unwashed, there're milk stains on her top, and she's making soft snoring noises. But she's never looked more beautiful.

Motherhood suits my wife, and as soon as she's ready, I'll put another baby in her belly.

I'm addicted to the milky smell of Mia's head, the feel of her tiny body pressed against mine, and the way she settles against me, taking comfort from the fact that I'm here for her.

With one last look at Amy, I quietly close the door and head downstairs.

I'll let her sleep while she can, and since I need to keep moving or Mia will wake up, I get started on the housework, cleaning up the dinner dishes from last night.

Yeah, the house is a mess, my wife is exhausted, and I haven't had time to keep myself in shape since Mia arrived. I'm permanently tired, and we're eating takeout far more than we should. But I wouldn't have it any other way.

Tony may feel smug that this isn't his life, but I feel lucky. I have an incredible wife and a beautiful daughter. I wouldn't swap it for the world.

* * *

WHAT TO READ NEXT

PROTECTING HIS EX-WIFE

When I made my vows, it was forever...

Caroline may be my ex-wife, but she's still mine to protect and love until death do us part.

She may have moved on, but that doesn't stop me from keeping her safe.

She thinks the military turned me into a monster.

But when her new husband and business partner turns out to be a threat, I'll do whatever it takes to protect her—even if it means becoming the monster she believes I am.

But will it ruin any shot I have of a second chance with my ex-wife?

Protecting His Ex-Wife is a second-chance romance featuring an OTT protective ex-military security guard and his curvy ex-wife.

Keep reading for an exclusive excerpt or go to:
mybook.to/SSProtectingHisExWife

PROTECTING HIS EX-WIFE

CHAPTER ONE

Caroline

My forehead sinks into my palm, and I squeeze my tired eyes shut as I listen to the loans specialist on the other end of the phone tell me why they won't be going ahead with my application.

"But I can pay. If I could just take a three-month payment break at the start of the loan..."

Even I hate the desperation in my voice, and it's clearly not doing anything to convince the woman on the other end of the line that they should lend me money.

"I'm sorry, Mrs. Leveson. We can't help you."

The voice is firm, and I know there's no point in trying to change her mind.

"Thank you for your time," I mumble before ending the call and slamming my phone down on the desk.

My mug jumps, and cold coffee sloshes over the rim. I watch it trickle down the side of the "Girl Boss" mug, leaving a muddy trail through the cheerful pink block writing.

With a heavy sigh, I open my laptop. I've filled out numerous online loan applications in the last two days and gotten more rejections than I care to count. I can't handle any more calls with sympathetic but firm loan specialists today.

It's time to turn my attention to the task I've been putting off all day. There are forty-three unread emails in my inbox. I scan the bold subject lines.

"Where's my order?" "Missing order." And the passive aggressive "Thanks for ruining my health kick."

My fingers are shaking as I open the first one. I've been dreading this all day, but I can no longer ignore my angry customers.

The first email is pleasant, simply wondering where their order is. They remind me that the money has already left their account and they paid for three day delivery, but that was two weeks ago.

I hit "reply" and paste the template response I created last week when I realized how far that asshole ex-business partner and soon-to-be ex-husband had ripped me off. It explains that we're having supplier issues and I'll send their order out as soon as I can.

I spend the next two hours replying to emails, trying to appease my upset customers, some of whom I've met personally at events, and pray that none of them ask for a refund.

By the time I've finished replying to the emails, my eyes are strained and my neck stiff. I get out of my chair and stretch, rolling my shoulders as I walk to the window.

My home office is on the second floor. I spend a moment looking at the palm trees that line the road, swaying in the wind. My shirt sticks to my body in the heat, but I daren't put the air conditioning on. I'm not sure I'll be able to pay the rent next week. I don't want to add any unnecessary bills.

A wave of bitterness rises my throat. This was supposed to be my time. After raising my daughter practically on my own, it was my time to finally do what I wanted in life.

The move to LA, launching the food supplement business, the new husband.

But look how it turned out. A failing business, a crook for a husband, and now it's sticky hot and I'm stuck in my home office trying to get myself out of this mess.

I push myself against the open window, letting the faint breeze sweep across my brow. My eyes close and I strain my ears, listening for the sounds of the ocean.

I'm only a few blocks away, but I may as well be inland. The only noise I hear is the continuous flow of traffic that never seems to stop. So much for the LA dream.

When I open my eyes, I catch sight of a dark car parked across the road. My heart leaps into my throat.

What if it's him? What if it's Paul, my ex-husband?

Fear grips me, and I step back from the window, my heart hammering in my chest. My ex took my money and he ruined my business, but that wasn't enough. He said if I reported him, he'd kill me and come for my daughter.

Yeah, nice guy I got involved with.

With my blood thumping in my ears, I peer around the side of the curtain to take a better look at the car.

The window is open a crack, and through the top of it I catch a glimpse of a bald head—a large bald, shiny head that I'd recognize anywhere.

The panic subsides, and my heart slows in relief.

It's a different ex who's scoping out my place. Because, yeah, in addition to having a failed business, I have not one but two failed marriages.

You're supposed to be wiser as you get older, but at thirty-eight, I'm more of a hot mess than I was at eighteen.

The relief that it's Tony in the car and not Paul is soon replaced by indignation.

Ever since I accidentally let slip that Paul had left in bad circumstances, Tony think's it's his duty to come down here to LA whenever he can to keep an eye on me as if I can't look after myself.

It would be sweet if it wasn't so hypocritical. For all the years we were married, he was in the military. He left me alone more days than he was home. I had our daughter alone. I practically raised her alone.

I knew when I married Tony that he was going into the military. After all, it had always been his dream. But I wasn't prepared for the life of a military wife.

We always knew we'd get married one day, but when I found out I was pregnant at eighteen, it sped things up. Tony had already enlisted, and he wanted me to be looked after as a military wife. He wanted to know I wasn't on my own when he was away.

And I was looked after. But it was lonely.

I hated Tony being away so much. I hated that I was raising Amy on my own. I tried for twelve years to make it work, but finally Tony agreed to a divorce.

Now he thinks he can come down here and stake out my place like he's on some military mission. Well, I'm not his responsibility anymore.

After the divorce, I moved out of the military compound. I got a house for me and Amy and focused on raising our daughter.

I started a health supplement business on the side, but it only flourished once Amy turned eighteen and I had more time to focus on the business.

Tony was back for good by then, so I figured he could be there for Amy. It was my time. She moved in with her dad, and I moved to LA with Paul.

Everyone said LA is where I need to be for health supplements, and it's only a few hours from the Sunset Coast but it feels like a world away.

I miss Amy. I miss the ocean. And if there's a part of me that still misses Tony, I keep it buried deep inside me. That ship has sailed.

So when I see him out my window, keeping watch again, all I feel is anger. He wasn't there when I needed him, and now he's here when I don't want him.

I march down the stairs and out of the front door. As I cross the road, he winds his window down with a sheepish look.

"What are you doing here, Tony?"

Available from Amazon or visit:
mybook.to/SSProtectingHisExWife

GET YOUR FREE BOOK

Sign up to the Sadie King mailing list for a FREE book!

You'll be the first to hear about exclusive offers, bonus content and all the news from Sadie King.

To claim your free book visit:
www.authorsadieking.com/free

BOOKS BY SADIE KING

Sunset Coast

Underground Crows MC

Sunset Security

Men of the Sea

The Thief's Lover

The Henchman's Obsession

The Hitman's Redemption

Maple Springs

Men of Maple Mountain

All the Single Dads

Candy's Café

Small Town Sisters

Kings County

Kings of Fire

King's Cops

For a full list of titles check out the Sadie King website

www.authorsadieking.com

ABOUT THE AUTHOR

Sadie King is a USA Today Best Selling Author of short instalove romance.
She lives in New Zealand with her ex-military husband and raucous young son.

Follow Sadie King on BookBub to get an alert whenever she has a new release, preorder, or discount!

www.bookbub.com/authors/sadie-king

www.authorsadieking.com

Printed in Great Britain
by Amazon